Pop Does the Bop!

by Liza Charlesworth • illustrated by Doug Jones

SCHOLASTIC INC.

New York • Toronto • London • Auckland • Sydney
Mexico City • New Delhi • Hong Kong • Buenos Aires

Designed by Grafica, Inc.
ISBN: 978-0-545-68621-1
Copyright © 2009 by Lefty's Editorial Services.
All rights reserved. Published by Scholastic Inc.
SCHOLASTIC, LET'S LEARN READERS™, and associated logos are trademarks and/or registered trademarks of Scholastic Inc.

12 11 10 9 8 7 6 5 4 3 2 1   68   15 16 17 18 19 20/0

Printed in China.

The Op Family

What Is a Word Family?
A word family is a group of words that rhyme and share the same spelling pattern, such as *Pop, top,* and *bop.* Read this story to learn more *–op* words!

Meet **Pop**.
Pop is a member of the **Op** family.

Pop Op loves
to put on his **top** hat...

and do the **bop**!

Pop just won't **stop**.

Pop dances with Grandma **Op**.
Bop, bop, bop!

Pop dances with a **mop**.
Bop, bop, bop!

Pop dances in a toy **shop**.
Bop, bop, bop!

Pop dances on a **hilltop**.
Bop, **bop**, **bop**!

Pop dances in the rain.
Bop, **bop**, **bop**!

Pop hips and **hop**s with every **drop**.
Plop, plop, plop!

Uh-oh, here comes a **cop**.
Can the **cop** get **Pop** to **stop**?

Nope.
But **Pop** CAN get the **cop** to **bop**.
Bop, bop, bop!

Word Family House

Point to the *-op* word in each room and read it aloud.

hop	cop	lop
bop	top	mop
crop	Pop	drop
plop		chop
shop		stop

Word Family Match

Read each definition. Then go to the raindrops and put your finger on the right -*op* word.

Definitions

1. a kind of dance

2. a store

3. a small jump

4. the opposite of bottom

5. a police officer

shop

top

hop

bop

cop

-op words

Word Family Maze

Help Pop find the cop. Put your finger on BEGIN. Then follow the trail of -*op* words to get to the END.

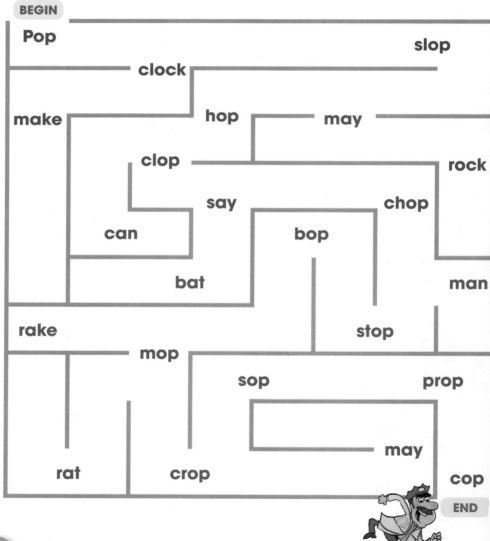

BEGIN

Pop   slop

clock

make   hop   may

clop   rock

say   chop

can   bop

bat   man

rake   stop

mop

sop   prop

may

rat   crop   cop

END